THE THREE BILLY GOATS BUENOS

BY **Susan Middleton Elya**

ILLUSTRATED BY **Miguel Ordóñez**

xz

E

putnam

G. P. PUTNAM'S SONS

To my sisters, Barb and Nancy —S.M.E.

To Lucia —M.O.

G. P. PUTNAM'S SONS
an imprint of Penguin Random House LLC, New York

Visit us online at penguinrandomhouse.com

Library of Congress Cataloging-in-Publication Data
Names: Elya, Susan Middleton, 1955– author. | Ordóñez, Miguel, 1976– illustrator.
Title: The three billy goats buenos / Susan Middleton Elya; illustrated by Miguel Ordóñez.
Description: New York: G. P. Putnam's Sons, [2020]
Summary: "A rhyming twist on the classic tale in which the goats help fix what is making the troll so grumpy in order to cross the bridge.
Incorporates Spanish words and includes a glossary"—Provided by publisher.
Identifiers: LCCN 2018052516 (print) | LCCN 2018057084 (ebook) | ISBN 9780399547409 (ebook) | ISBN 9780399547393 (hardcover)
Subjects: | CYAC: Stories in rhyme. | Goats—Fiction. | Trolls—Fiction. | Helpfulness—Fiction.
Classification: LCC PZ8.3.E514 (ebook) | LCC PZ8.3.E514 Thr 2020 (print) | DDC [E]—dc23
LC record available at https://lccn.loc.gov/2018052516

Manufactured in China by RR Donnelley Asia Printing Solutions Ltd.
ISBN 9780399547393

3 5 7 9 10 8 6 4 2

Design by Marikka Tamura. Text set in Atelier Sans ITC Std.
The art was done in pencil, collage, and digital.

(los) **amigos** (*ah MEE goce*) friends (all male or a mix of male and female)

ay (*I*) oh

buenos (*BWEH noce*) good (plural)

(la) **cabeza** (*kah BEH sah*) head

(los) **cabritos** (*kah BREE toce*) little goats

(la) **cara** (*KAH rah*) face

delicioso (*deh lee SYOE soe*) delicious

(los) **desayunos** (*deh sah YOO noce*) breakfasts

después (*dehs PWEHS*) after, later

(los) **dientes** (*DYEHN tehs*) teeth

Dos (*DOSE*) Two

el, los (*EHL, LOCE*) the (masculine singular and plural)

(el) **elefante** (*eh leh FAHN teh*) elephant

(la) **espina** (*ehs PEE nah*) thorn

(las) **frutas** (*FROO tahs*) fruit

(el) **gigante** (*hee GAHN teh*) giant

(el) **hermano** (*ehr MAH noe*) brother

(las) **hierbas** (*YEHR bahs*) herbs

inteligente (*een teh leh HEHN teh*) intelligent

la, las (*LAH, LAHS*) the (feminine singular and plural)

(los) **labios** (*LAH byoce*) lips

(el) **lado** (*LAH doe*) side

(la) **lágrima** (*LAH gree mah*) tear

(las) **manzanas** (*mahn SAH nahs*) apples

mi, mis (*MEE, MEECE*) my (singular and plural)

(el) **momentito** (*moe mehn TEE toe*) little moment

ningunos (*neen GOO noce*) none

Número (*NOO meh roe*) Number

(los) **ojos** (*OE hoce*) eyes

prado (*PRAH doe*) meadow

(el) **puente** (*PWEHN teh*) bridge

(el) **río** (*RREE oe*) river

sabroso (*sah BROE soe*) tasty

Tres (*TREHS*) Three

Uno (*OO noe*) One

(la) **vecina** (*veh SEE nah*) neighbor

(la) **voz** (*VOCE*) voice

There once were three goats, a brotherly trio.
They needed to crisscross a fast-moving **río**.

But under the bridge lived a grumpy **gigante**
with tootsies as big as a small **elefante**.

Troll's **ojos** were glowing. Her nose was a hook.
She stopped kids from crossing with one scary look.

With three heads together, a mission was planned
to get past the grumpiest troll in the land!

The smallest goat, **Uno**, so **inteligente**,
clip-clopped right up to the edge of **el puente**.

"Hey!" roared the troll, her giant head bobbing.

"You have some nerve, and soon you'll be sobbing."

"Please," said the hoof-shaking tiny **cabrito**,
"may I go by in a short **momentito**?"

"How many creatures can pass me? **¡Ningunos!**
You kids will be part of **mis desayunos!**"

"Wait!" said the little goat. "I'm not **sabroso**.
Try my big brother. He's so **delicioso**!

"In fact, my small bones will stick in your **dientes**.
Wait till the bigger goat reaches your **puente**.

"He's headed this way to that meadow of grass."
The troll licked her **labios**. "Fine, you may pass."

The little goat crossed to the bank's other **lado**,
then followed his nose to the lush, lovely **prado**.

Along came the second goat, **Número Dos**.

"Halt!" yelled the troll in her scritch-scratchy **voz**.

"My meal is before me, here for the taking!

See these big chompers? Why aren't you shaking?"

"Wait!" said the middle goat. "I'm not **sabroso**. Try my big brother. He's so **delicioso**!"

The troll rubbed her chin, both whiskered and warty. "I heard a rumor that *you'd* taste good, shorty."

The goat shook his spotted **cabeza**. "Not me!
These spots will taste bitter. I'm the worst of the three!"

The troll licked her **labios**. "Fine, you may pass!"
The goat hurried off to the clover and grass.

He joined his **hermano**.
The two butted heads.
They frolicked and romped
like true quadrupeds.

Then next came the biggest goat, **Número Tres**.
*If the troll lets me by, what will she eat **después**?*

And why's she so grumpy? **Tres** wanted to know.
His gentle eyes noticed the gal's swollen toe!

Stuck to her foot was a long, sharp **espina**.
"¡**Ay!** That must hurt you a lot, **mi vecina**!"

A big, salty **lágrima** fell from her eye.
"No one has noticed. You're the first guy!"

The goat called his brothers.
"This troll needs a remedy.
Please gather **hierbas**
to soothe her extremity."

Goat **Tres** pulled the thorn. He used his big **dientes**. That gal was the happiest troll of all **puentes**.

The others found herbs, mashed them up with their teeth,
returned to her foot, put the paste underneath.

Next they picked **frutas** in an orchard nearby.
"A gift of **manzanas**?" she said. "I might cry."

The troll's scary **cara** stopped looking so mean,
and she'd wave to the three as they crossed to the green.

"Pass, young **cabritos**, and don't pay a toll.
We're all **amigos**," said their new friend, the troll.